[Lil Blæk Book]

All the Long Stories Short

TS Hawkins

iUniverse, Inc.
Bloomington

Lil Blæk Book
All the Long Stories Short

iUniverse books may be ordered through booksellers or by contacting:

iUniverse
1663 Liberty Drive
Bloomington, IN 47403
www.iuniverse.com
1-800-Authors (1-800-288-4677)

First printed by Wordclay August 24, 2011

Cover Design by TS Hawkins

ISBN: 978-1-4759-7553-6 (sc)
ISBN: 978-1-4759-7554-3 (e)

Printed in the United States of America

iUniverse rev. date: 2/6/2013

[Lil Blæk Book]

All the Long Stories Short

color me beautiful|wrap me in crayolas big box|hues cascading down the soul|render rainbow boundless|as it should be|without question|color me beautiful|wrap me in crayolas big box|hues cascading down the soul|render rainbow boundless|as it should be|without question| color me beautiful|wrap me in crayolas big box|hues cascading down the soul|render rainbow boundless|as it should be|without question|color me beautiful|wrap me in crayolas big box|hues cascading down the soul|render rainbow boundless|as it should be|without question| color me beautiful|wrap me in crayolas big box|hues cascading down the soul|render rainbow boundless|as it should be|without question|color me beautiful|wrap me in crayolas big box|hues cascading down the soul|render rainbow boundless|as it should be|without question| color me beautiful|wrap me in crayolas big box|hues cascading down the soul|render rainbow boundless|as it should be|without question|color me beautiful|wrap me in crayolas big box|hues cascading down the soul|render rainbow boundless|as it should be|without question| color me beautiful|wrap me in crayolas big box|hues cascading down the soul|render rainbow boundless|as it should be|without question| color me beautiful|wrap me in crayolas big box|hues cascading down the soul|render rainbow boundless|as it should be|without question|color me beautiful|wrap me in crayolas big box|hues cascading down the soul|render rainbow boundless|as it should be|without question| color me beautiful|wrap me in crayolas big box|hues cascading down the soul|render rainbow boundless|as it should be|without question| color me beautiful|wrap me in crayolas big box|hues cascading down the soul|render rainbow boundless|as it should be|without question|color me beautiful|wrap me in crayolas big box|hues cascading down the soul|render rainbow boundless|as it should be|without question|color me beautiful|wrap me in crayolas big box|hues cascading down the soul|render rainbow boundless|as it should be|without question| color me beautiful|wrap me in crayolas big box|hues cascading down the soul|render rainbow boundless|as it should be|without question| color me beautiful\wrap me in crayolas big box\hues cascading down the soul\render rainbo

OTHER TITLES BY TS HAWKINS

***

Sugar Lumps and Black Eye Blues
Confectionately Yours
Mahogany Nectar
The Hotel Haikus
Running Still Water

*****UPCOMING RELEASES*****

Black Suga: diary of a troublesome teenager
Poetry Schmo-etry
A Woman Scorned is a Woman Blessed
On My Knees Too Long: Prayers, Proverbs & Poems to GOD
Becoming Saturn: Counting Backwards from 60-30

Books/CDs available for purchase at all major online retailers

&

www.tspoetics.com

bawled inside composition

the most

honest words I've ever

written…

~ Lil Blæk Book

ACKNOWLEDGEMENTS

***

For what lies ahead

TABLE OF CONTENTS

***

PROLOGUE

Iris In Wonderland

***

Nightmares become day mares
That stampede through glazed cortex streets
Gas lamps Morse code danger in shuddering foot trails
Heart pounds to rhythms unrehearsed
Praying, pleading to pray again
The re-do in slumber-land is REM on pause
Hiccupped matrix scrambling insight with hindsight
Where nothings 20/20 when you turn out the lights
So, for sanity
Doze off with one eye open

[fu**h**k yu]

VII

fade to black
epic soliloquies render muted encores
act accordingly

VI

blue
the out of
you have conjured yourself from
attempting to make it a spectrum of mine

...swoon to grey shades...

VIII

rubber necking
streams of consciousness
red
read,
go faster
common sensual knowledge
belted in miles per horror
intoxicated in
yellows
yielding for naught
envy flashes
blinking
"told-you-so" tones
deafening to hindsight
knew adoring you was an accident
waiting to commence

XI

for real,
enough with the
malarkey.
all this
lust is unnecessary
end it

<u>II</u>

encased in death/still holding reigns/but this mare broke free years ago/only allowing bareback riders to gallop through what's left of this journey/"I click, Not Attending" to your eternal bed/for now, it's for the best

I

Fuck what you heard
You're obsurd

Somehow,
I'm the idiot for loving you

<u>IV</u>

time. when
every moment; devoted.
xylose adoration.
the past.

III

leaks
'tween
your
thighs
envy
evenly
leaving
sour
essences
clutched
throated
back
eroding
the
taste
of future serenity

IX

irked
hellfire stroking open wounds
quill ready to spurn the fabricated
spindled existence
weaved through jealous tales
how dare you make mockery of ink-lined sophistication
MY PEN HATES YOU
through Gerber beginnings
linguistically mastered your fractured sentence-tree
so what you won't do is babble on about what you are trying to be
by disrespecting your ancestry

XII

The devil
reincarnated its spirit
in the offspring of your half thoughts
living vicariously in erasure residue
watch you gather shavings
to nullify that your negative energy was positive
but you're...
poison picking-obsolete driven-noose dangling
yanking at every fiber of emotion
wet willy-ed my consciousness
with middle digit sophistication
stop mind fucking me
drowning in everything you never wanted
should have burnt your penmanship in lava's hell fire
struck the match on the womb
that helped create the you I can't stand
set inferno to the sperm and egg that fornicated the demon essence
allowed to jaunt
pontificate righteousness with an inflamed tongue of super ego-ed halitosis
with upside down pressed palms
pray that realization pistol whips the fester bound lies oozing from your mouth piece
in other words...
fuck the part of you that's actually human
you don't deserve to be whole

V

smell foreign taste-buds on thighs
death-rattle moans scale vibrato tombstones
rigor mortis sex-
stain anything worth living for

XIII

Embrace...
Elevated consciousness of falsified energy
Lie next to lies told to categorize a nature of unnatural humanity
Existing between cosmic space of osmosis and bi-labial demise
Trusting such verve was fatal to the soul
Bowing out to serendipitous melancholy
Unplugging receptors stationed at heart's portal
Who knew love was spelled
"F-I-C-K-L-E"
Static noise is more comforting
Earthly scum
Most times signified with lackluster performances of another
Won't disgrace scum
It does its job

X

exuding ringlet intelligence
wishing to finger through brilliance
weaving through phallic disdain
cumming to the conclusion...

naturally can't stand you!

XIV

like molten lava/your apology singes my chest cavity/scorching the ability to find the truth in anything else/never should have let you in/but with this lesson/learned that fertile soil lies under devastation/know now that no one is entitled to my love

[ˈpol-i-tiks]

XVIII

quadroon tycoon ballrooms
where melancholy history
repeats hollow auto-tunes of blistering submission
raping future with dip & song
diphthong waist line
in base line segregated hem
nulls beauty in Mason Dixon stale mate

XVI

My love is too "just enough" to have thrown back in my face/to face the intelligence you seem to think I don't possess/as if the hot bed of mistakes didn't last long enough for you to remember my name/for when you told the story nonlinear to the truth embedded in the nape of your neck/you've created spookhouse in my soul/& I don't get to receive a paycheck after the credits have rolled/a bold move for someone once afraid of the darkness/where cellar beds were flat-mates/sharing fags/haggling tales/doctoring forget me knots in key slots doubling as sympathy/now you hold the key & refuse to open doors/all you are good for is dangling last hopes out blockbuster windows/like the yellow coward you are/nightstand hiding behind $12.50/I could have masturbated with more urgency/this is why we considered suicide/because you already left our rainbow out to die

XIX

pungent post-mortem phalanges
scan/stroke/grieve
birthing death whispers
in morning dew carbonation
"should of killed myself when he stuck it in me"
afterthought
could have been foreseen
in prophylactic tactics
blue born prints
map new journeys

...happy birthday irony...

XXI

the Statue of Liberty
never thought she would stand
for Statutes of Limitations
bowed heads
not due to reverence
but shame
for justice unkept

XV

done time in dark spaces that bonded bails and pardons couldn't save the misunderstanding that took up cot in my consciousness/prisoner to the ghosts of the past/freed the mind by earning degree/this caged bird has begun to sing/finally educated enough to write thesis's truth/but you can't accept the paperwork for it was attained behind bars/will the soul ever catch a break

XXII

I pledge alliance to my doubts
And the united fronts that I put forward
To the autonomy I can't afford
One spirit; under siege
Undeliverable
With no justice after all

['let-ərs]

XLI

Dear Fool:

iTouch-ed you in order to find peace within myself only to discover that you aren't worth technological menstruation that leaks in the fold of my iPad.
iDock you in the outskirts of my consciousness.

XLIII

Dear Fool:

When I was shaped like an orange you treated me like strange fruit.
Now, that my new figure has caught your eye, your cocktail is extra syrupy.
Get your fruit out my bowl!

XLII

Dear Fool:

My apple bottom never wanted to coast away to your banana's republic.
Please don't flatter yourself into believing I'm captivated by minuscule compliments.
Fall into the gap of my short term acknowledgment.

XLVI

Dear "Friend":

You think you call the shots in this relationship,
until I don't pick up the phone.

<u>XL</u>

Dear Fool:

I asked you for change.
In my hand you placed a mirror…
guess I own the title now?

[luhr]

<u>XXVII</u>

periwinkle
crimson
blues
red
clear
amethyst
grey
violets

XXVI

notebook doodles
portray what
words cannot...

<u>XXV</u>

I never told you,
but you remind me of a distant relative
spirit kindredly adjacent to the fears I've left behind.

Attracted to your past mistakes

I find myself letting history repeat itself

XXIX

hum
you
lullabies
use
last
moments
peace
to
rock
you
to
sleep
because
you deserve it

<u>XXXIII</u>

adverbs and nouns
play skipping stones
making ripples on the tongue
taste every sway
metaphors drip-drop in lingual pond
to be a lily cumming off the vibratious aftermath
is an ichthyologist dream...

...though, shallow water scares me...

XXI

live
lust
launder
lead
loathe
like
leave
linger
lost
liberate
libate
listen
lean

"s'il vous plaît revenir à moi"

XXXII

for assorted queers
who considered loneliness
when relationships become too much...

...honorable...

XXXIX

You are sunshine and rain
Sex on the beach
Long islands rum running
Draped in everything dark and stormy
You are dangerously beautiful
And handsomely divine
Time after time
Bringing myself in the womb of your wisdom
Danger always felt sweeter with you

XXXV

Dripping ecstasy from nectar rimmed labia
Bilaterally fringed
Tongued whisked on the glory soon to be labeled delicacy
You're more than mere garnish
A savory sip supple satisfaction
Making "lip smacking good"
wish it birthed seasonings unfettered from common budded tastes
A cuisine soul filling
Body bursting orgasmic belches
Manifesting space to consumè gelee's du jour
Palette-able encore
Rip roaring herbs and spices to prance on chef's platter-ed specials
"Pardon! Garçon…serve me some her…again"

XXXVI

Mint juleps with Sunday veranda
Side sipping nature's tea cupped morning dew
Sun dipped whispers penning olive branches in the quilled honey suckle
Piece peace in afternoon's dusk luncheon
Conducting ritual
Never once leaving lounge chairs
Lingering in evening's cashmere wind song
Scribbling a setting day in rosemary kisses drizzled in thyme
Could this be happiness?

XXIII

backbone hums tunes
unstrummed by no other|scalin quiverin vertebrae|
maestro play those notes forever|
soul beats|this is the way ♥ feels

XXXVIII

I don't sleep
on your side
of my bed
for fear that when you return
you think I've replaced you

<u>XXVIII</u>

foot
s
            t
                        e
                                    p
                                                s
hand holding throughout becoming
            s
            t
            e
            e
            p
never letting go

[despite]

XXXVII

love smells like burnt remnants left behind
when uttered words

"it's not you it's me"

ignites molten flames to torch anything
pressed flesh had the luxury of caressing
love smells like blues skies and grey days
mating mauve afternoons
in the park where I allowed you to borrow my womb
signing sweet somethings over hymen's braille
never knowing you were more fluent in other languages
waiting for the next to season fair-weather taste buds of
consciousness
where rain clouds hail storm

"it's not you it's me"

XXXIV

bittersweet
lick past to finite confection
saccharine glaze present
gift wrap in assorted nuts
voraciously dipped for punishment

XXIX

broken hearted
living with it
not for tortured soul anecdotes
hate notes
corkless wine strokes
but to let the pieces fall where they may
for when the chips are down
they become the solution to someone's else puzzle
love comes in all forms
and meant to be shared!

XXIV

color me beautiful|wrap me in crayolas big box|
hues cascading down the soul|render rainbow boundless|
as it should be|without question

EPILOGUE

Ananphora Adoration

***

I love like
summer nights baking on dawn's fallen follies

I love like
I wish I knew what it could possibly be

I love like
hyperboles conjured in memorandum of the you I never met

I love like
reality's daydreams

I love like
apex-ed surges generated penning doodled last names together like
first bitten teenagers

I love like
I thought I was supposed to

I love like
the pseudonyms given to crimson stemmed roses

I love like
I wish I knew what it could possibly be

ABOUT THE AUTHOR

***

TS Hawkins is overjoyed to produce her first collection of short poems. After penning the final words to place in this book, she realized that brevity is not as simple as it seems.

When she is not sitting in front of the computer, she is performing with the **Authors Under 30 Book Tour** and promoting literacy in public schools. She will be published in her first anthology called *Verseadelphia. Verseadelphia* is an anthology of Philadelphia's African American Poets and Spoken Word Artists during the 20th - 21st Century. She is honored to be in the same collection as her idols Sonia Sanchez and Ursula Rucker. Hawkins is elated that this publication will be a learning tool for the Philadelphia public school system. Recently, she was a featured poet on two CD compilations by ***Drexel University's Late Night Series*** and ***Lady M Productions: Arts4TheCause***. Crowned the *PBGP Poetry Slam Champion* in 2009 and a judge for the past couple years, she is thrilled that her work is taking shape while inspiring individuals from all lifestyles.

A Temple University Poetry as Performance Alumni, she has written three publications titled **Sugar Lumps and Black Eye Blues**, **Confectionately Yours** and **Mahogany Nectar** which have had rave reviews in print and radio media. It is with hope **Lil Blæk Book: *All the Long Stories Short*** and her new teen publication **Black Suga: diary of a troublesome teenager** will follow in the latter books' successes. Selections from her books have been featured on: 107.9 WRNB (*Whispers in the Dark with Tiffany Bacon)*, LP Spoken Word Tour, Brown Girl Radio: *a Cure for the Common*, Da Block, WRTI 90.1 FM (*The Bridge with J. Michael Harrison*), Studio Luna, Improv Café, Temple University, Aspire Arts, NBC 10, Moonstone: 100 Poets Reading, NateBrown Entertainment, The Liacouras Center, Tree House Books, The Bowery, Warmdaddy's, Jus Words, NJ Performing Arts Center, T Bar, Verbal Roots, The NAACP, The REC, Lyrical Playground, Lincoln University, The Pleazure Principle, Bar 13, Robin's

Bookstore, umuvme Radio, First Person Arts, The RED Lounge for AIDS Awareness, Women's Ink, Lady M Events, The Painted Bride, So 4Real, Charis Books and Dr. Sonia Sanchez Literacy Night. Next, she is trying her hand at playwriting while infusing puppetry into her poetry!

Currently, she produces and operates her own radio show on PR Radio Station. Hawkins also blogs for *If You Give A Girl A Pen*, a website that gives woman writers a positive forum to enhance writing fundamentals!

For bookings and detailed information:
www.TSPoetics.com